Tapestry

A story of the healing of the soul

a novella
Hunter D. Darden

Illustrations and dustjacket design
by Martha Neaves

Darden, Hunter D.
Tapestry-A story of the healing of the soul

Library of Congress Catalog Number 2003095156
ISBN 0-9653729-4-4
[1.Grief—Fiction. 2 Death—Fiction 3.Christian
Life—Fiction 4. Hope—Fiction.]

Printed and bound in South Korea through Pacifica
Communications

Published by Sunfleur Publications, Inc.

To my friends who sat beside me while I healed

In loving memory of my sister, Fran, my brother, Charlie, and my father, Dr. Council Dudley

...until we meet to laugh and love again....

Tapestry is a tale of loss and healing that invites the reader to travel with the main character and experience redemption. Readers who have lost loved ones and questioned God's presence in the process will find comfort here.

Dr. Robert R. Shelton, Psychologist
Pitt Memorial Hospital, Greenville, NC

I was profoundly touched by *Tapestry*. It was impressive the way Olivia processed the three losses simultaneously. Each new loss inevitably brings up past losses. We have to work through the past, as well as, the present. I will have yet another tool in helping those who are grieving. *Tapestry* is a gift to those who grieve.

Jane Hill Riley, Ph.D.
Marriage and Family Therapist

Hunter Darden has used *Tapestry* to work through her own grief and suffering and in so doing has provided a model for her readers.

The Reverend Pat Earle, Ph.D.
Trinity Episcopal Church
Statesville, NC

Foreword

"Why do bad things happen to good people?" Public figures from the biblical Job to Rabbi Kushner, along with every other human being who has endured a senseless tragedy, wrestle with this question. We don't understand natural disasters or deadly accidents or catastrophic illnesses. We want our lives and the lives of those we love to have meaning. We want goodness to be rewarded by long life and prosperity. We want life to be fair. Above all, we want God to take care of us. And when our illusions about life's fairness are shattered by reality, we question if God is truly all-loving and all-powerful-if God even exists.

The death of her beloved sister wrenched up memories of earlier sorrows and precipitated Hunter Darden into a struggle with the mysteries of God and of God's role in our lives. In *Tapestry*, she weaves a fabric of fiction and truth that poignantly depicts a journey through the depths and into the light of healing. This is a book that I expect will find an audience both among those who enjoy a "good read" and those who are seeking answers to their own tough questions.

Reverend Dale Walker

The Weaver

My Life is but a weaving
Between my God and me.
I may not choose the colors
He knows what they should be.

For He can view the pattern
Upon the upper side,
While I can see it only
On this, the under side.

Sometimes He weaveth sorrow,
Which seemeth strange to me;
But I will trust His judgment,
And work on faithfully;

'Tis He who fills the shuttle
He knows just what is best,
So I shall weave in earnest
And leave with Him the rest.

The dark threads are as needful
In the Weaver's skillful hand
As the thread of gold and silver
In the pattern He has planned.

At last, when Life is ended,
With Him I shall abide,
Then I shall view the pattern
Upon the upper side;

Then I shall know the reason
Why pain, with joy entwined,
Was woven in the fabric
Of life, that God designed.

Anonymous

A Single Strand

'Wherever you go, there you are. Wasn't that what my father used to say? It was something like that... wasn't it? i think...maybe? If only i had listened then,' Olivia thought.

i'm ready to listen now...

If only...i wish...It's too late now...

Olivia's thoughts trailed off as she squeezed her eyes way too tightly. She pictured herself as a child in the room she shared with her sister, Rachael. Olivia cherished reliving the feeling of drifting off to sleep at night while listening to the hushed tones of her parents across the hall discussing their day. An occasional laugh could be heard. The soothing sounds of content camaraderie would waft through into Olivia's heart and soul leaving an eternal imprint.

It was comforting.

It was peaceful.

It was safe.

'If i could just recapture that feeling…that feeling from a time when the world felt all right because your Daddy made it feel that way…to a time when there was order, purpose and safety where nothing bad ever happened,' she thought. Olivia was beginning to feel her eyelids vibrate from trying to ignite the memories too fiercely.

'i just need to hold on a minute more,' she thought. She recalled the good night game she and Rachael had played as children. They appropriately called it "Laugh In The Pillow" because that's all there was to it. They laughed in their pillows to the point of raucousness until their Daddy would inevitably come in and say, "I don't want to hear another peep out of you girls!"

Olivia smiled to herself as she relived the moment when, as he was shutting the door, she and Rachael would shout out in silly unison, "Peep!" They knew that in spite of his sternness, he was actually finding his girls' antics entertaining.

'What was it Rachael used to say? It was something about imagination being better than intelligence. It was something like that...i think...maybe? If only i had listened then,' she thought.

i'm ready to listen now...

If only...i wish...It's too late now...

As a distraction from her thoughts, Olivia picked up a magazine. The little, yellow house on the cover caught her attention. It was charming with its white columns and a veranda style porch. There was a tire swing hanging from the limb of a giant oak tree that brought back childhood memories of innocent fun. She was taken back to a time when life was carefree, before the eclipse of her life began. To round out the perfect picture of delightfulness, there was a garden full of blooming flowers beckoning to be picked.

'What is it my mother says about planting flowers? It's something about using your time to plant your own garden, so you can be a better and more interesting bloom. Something like that…i think… maybe?' Olivia wondered.

i'm ready to listen now… It's not too late…

That charming, little, yellow house conjured up the image that happy things happened on the inside. It struck her that she had been pretending to live the life this past year of a charming, little, yellow house where it "appeared" happy things happened on the inside. But how can life be a charming, little, yellow house ever again when you've heard the words, "She will die soon after we take her off life support?"

Olivia thought to herself, 'That is the moment the pretending begins, the façade takes shape, hope becomes hopelessness and god becomes a little "g" to me.'

In Olivia's mind, god seems to have packed up his suitcases and moved out of the charming, little, yellow house…

Olivia's Journal

Someone told me once that we are a composite of all the people who have loved us. Therefore, when we lose someone we love, an important part of our identity is taken away. i suppose i will feel like a little "i" until i can recapture that important part of me that was lost. i know that rediscovering one's self is a lengthy process.

i tried to pray again today. The words felt rote and uninspired. i am disconnected from god. i can't believe i spelled god with a little "g", but he doesn't feel like a big "G" to me somehow. Interestingly, it goes hand in hand with my little "i" existence. god and i are quite a pair in our "littleness" it would seem. god will just have to be happy being a little "g" for now. If god is as understanding as i've been taught, then he will have to be patient with me.   i am disillusioned by his lack of response to my prayers and the prayers of many others to heal my sister.

i'll   have to think about that tomorrow... i suppose that is why my mother calls me Scarlet O'Hara when   i talk of postponing concerns.   Procrastinating emotions has always been a much easier route for me. god must procrastinate, too.   Is god a Scarlet O'Hara? Did he hear our prayers, but he put it on the back burner?   Or did god just "drop the ball" altogether?

Why does a "god of goodness" sabotage our lives by taking away people we love?

How can i be grateful to a god who would allow this kind of sadness for all of us?

i heard the most comforting sound on my walk this morning. It was the cooing of a mourning dove. It brought back a rush of memories of my father. He used to love to dove hunt. When i was a child, i innocently asked him, "Daddy, why did you kill those little birds?" He told my mother that he did not have any rational answer to my question. Consequently, he lost his desire to dove hunt, and he never killed another "little bird".

i can remember my father would make the sound of the dove by blowing in his cupped hands. In some curious way, i felt like my father was with me in spirit today.

i know that doves are a symbol of gentleness and peace. Perhaps, that would explain the gentle peacefulness i felt throughout my walk. i recall that Daddy used to say that doves are adaptable and that they feel most at home near people. i realize, that at this point in my life, i am struggling to be like an adaptable dove as i strive to be close to people again.

Mourning doves, also, have strong bonds with their mates. i wish i could be more like a dove. i'm sure jack wishes that, too. As much as i enjoy jack's company, he seems to be at the little "j" status along with god and me. i am as unable to express appreciation to jack as i am to god, even though i know how important they should

feel to me. The only difference is that jack
has never disappointed me.

god has.

jack told me he loved me again today. i
hope my silence doesn't push him away.
Sometimes, i pretend i don't hear him say
it. i want him and i don't want him all at
the same time. What if i love him and i lose
him?

i wish i could remember what it was my
father used to say about how to love...

Nevertheless, i was briefly comforted
today and that's all that matters. One day
at a time...one hour at a time...one minute
at a time...

i miss Rachael so...

Does god know that? Does god care?

Is god listening?

i'll think about that tomorrow...will god think about that tomorrow, too...or never?

The Entwining Threads

Olivia awoke to her usual morning thoughts. She knew that it would be yet another day of whys, wishful thinking, regrets, memories, unanswered questions and the exhaustion of pretending. She consciously found herself each morning putting on her makeup followed by the placement of "the mask". It was her protective shield for the day.

If i wear it just right, no one will know how much i'm hurting in my heart. i don't want pity. i want my life to feel normal again.

She recalled a conversation she had with a friend just last year. Olivia had told her that there was something about every part of the day that she enjoyed. That felt like a foreign thought to her now as she adjusted "the mask" for another day.

As Olivia stood in the warm, soothing shower, she felt anything but soothed. Jack crossed her mind fleetingly as she recalled their phone conversation from last night. He had wanted to cook dinner for her again. She turned him down with the old excuse of feeling tired and needing to go to bed early. Olivia was aware that the potential harm and pain from loss was too great for her to allow entrapment. Yet, in her heart, she knew she yearned to be engulfed by the comfort of his presence.

i enjoy him more and more every time i'm with him. i can't see someone i like this much on a regular basis. What if i show him i care about him and then i lose him?

Olivia hated that she was yanking around the emotions of a man who only wanted to be there as support for her. It made her feel even worse, because Jack was so good to her. She knew she would see him at work today and she would make the effort to patch up the hurt she had caused for him.

Olivia pulled on her jeans in casual preparation for her work at The Ragweed Garden. How interesting she thought that she was working at a place that so clearly described her state of mind- a limp rag and a weed among her peers. She felt like an alien of a sort, standing out and crying for nourishment in any form. Somehow, Olivia always found herself coming out of her morning doldrums in anticipation of the job she loved. The handling of the rich soil to planting the ugly seed that would eventually come to beautiful fruition gave her momentary, pleasant thoughts. It was the simple hopefulness of good things to come that made her smile briefly.

As Olivia walked toward the nursery, she could hear the sounds of happy whistling. It meant Jack was already there.

i love his happy whistle.

She felt her heart soar, and then the typical repression with which she was all too familiar.

Jack was the landscape architect for The Ragweed Garden, as well as, the heart and soul of the nursery. He gave Olivia his grinned greeting not even vaguely letting on of his disappointment about dinner.

i love his sweet smile.

Olivia was just getting ready to say, "I'm sorry about last night." Jack touched her gently on the hand and preempted her by saying, "Don't even worry about it. It's okay."

"What's okay?" Olivia asked feeling slightly stunned by his sensitive perception.

"I read your face, baby," said Jack.

i love it when he calls me baby.

His incredible sweetness touched her once again. Regardless, Olivia hesitantly replied, "Can we just do it another night?"

Olivia walked away thinking how unfair their situation was for him. She knew he was worthy of someone who could give him all he deserved. Instead, Jack was on the receiving end of her pitiful tokens of limited time and very little energy. Olivia wondered how he could continue to be interested.

The beauty of Olivia's job was that it gave her mind permission to drift far, far away. Her soul would come along for the ride. As she was planting the jonquil bulbs, her pondering thoughts began drifting toward Jack.

When Olivia first began working at The Ragweed Garden, she noticed Jack immediately. He had a certain comforting aura that drew Olivia to him. His physical presence radiated strength and commanded attention. He was tall with a muscular build that made looking away difficult. He had brown, wavy hair that was haphazardly coiffed; however, it complimented the thrown together selection of his clothes. It only made his unpretentious casualness even more appealing to her. Olivia thought he was the happiest person she had ever met. Jack had a permanent crease around his mouth from the familiarity of smiling. She was even more drawn to his kind, brown eyes. Those eyes would practically invite her inside for a look through the windows of his soul. It was a sweet soul she soon discovered. His quick wit was indicative of his sharp mind which only drew her even deeper into those eyes.

Jack had asked her for a date on her second day of work. They had been dating ever since for the past year. Jack was full of eagerness and had no apprehension about their relationship. Olivia was full of apprehension and had no eagerness to rush the relationship in spite of caring about him. Olivia couldn't help but be drawn to his raw courage and openness to express his feelings toward her even though her responses were lackluster.

Olivia noticed that Jack would sometimes drift pensively to that same far away place where she visited so often. This was their underlying connection Olivia suspected. They didn't even need to speak of where their meandering minds had been. Olivia knew where Jack's mind was and why. Jack knew where Olivia's mind was and why.

Olivia's mother always told her that she would know many wonderful people throughout her lifetime, but only a few truly exceptional ones. She would say, "Be especially aware when you meet one. They will be the ones with the most lasting effects on you. They will make the difference in your life." Olivia knew from the beginning that she was in the presence of that "exceptional" person about which her mother had spoken.

Jack's happy whistle was the wonderful topping on this exceptional man. It was a whistle that nourished her like a warm bath. Olivia loved her work with the flowers, but she realized that she looked forward to hearing Jack's whistling even more than seeing the beauty of the flowers.

Olivia's initial assumption was that he had obviously grown up in a happy family full of love and privileges. Judging by his whistle, you would certainly think he had come from a family who had cherished him. She didn't know the true circumstances of Jack's life until a mutual friend who had known him in high school told her over lunch one day. Olivia discovered that his life did not warrant happy whistling because of his unparalleled odds that began at his birth.

Jack never knew the identity of his father. He was abandoned as a baby by his mother who was a prostitute. Therefore, the responsibility for Jack's love and care fell on his grandfather. He was an elderly World War II veteran living on a paltry pension. Jack and his grandfather lived together in a seedy, urban hotel room. Olivia's friend said that everyone in his class knew of his situation, but they refrained from teasing or judging him. She said that his whistling began in high school. Olivia surmised that his trademark whistling was the by-product of his innate happiness and his brave adaptation skills.

Some of the teachers who visited Jack's hotel room realized his dire situation. They were amazed over his academic achievements in spite of the lack of encyclopedias or other resources in that lonely hotel room. Surprisingly, Jack felt no pity for himself. He lived by fortitude and a complete self-acceptance.

The town's mothers became Jack's "mother". The support for Jack was proven when a large celebration was held in one of their homes for his sixteenth birthday. The event was attended by three-fourths of his class. They were his loyal friends who were smitten by the charm of a poor, but rich in spirit, whistling boy. Their attendance was reciprocity for his endearing nature that had effectively lifted their spirits through the years.

Jack's trademark was his well-worn green sweater that he undoubtedly washed in the hotel bathtub. It shrank to a size much too small for his body. Nevertheless, it was worn without complaint by him. Jack was respected by his class for his inner self and he was never teased by his fellow classmates for his lack of a stylish wardrobe.

Olivia's friend added that he was voted by the class to be an officer in each high school grade including president of his senior class. This did not surprise Olivia. She knew his friends must have been looking through those kind eyes into his sweet soul as she had.

Olivia thought to herself, 'Who wouldn't love a person who whistled happily all the time?'

After high school, Jack served in the military and was able to go to college on the GI Bill. He had always had a love for nature. Jack received a degree in landscape architecture which led him to The Ragweed Garden, the most outstanding nursery in the area.

Olivia was jolted out of her reverie when she heard Jack yell out, "How about dinner tonight?"

Yes! Yes! i'd love to come!

Olivia felt her heart lift. Successfully hiding her excitement, she merely said, "May I let you know later?"

What was it my father used to say about how to love?

i wasn't listening then... i'm ready to listen now...

Olivia's Journal

jack asked me to dinner again tonight. i admire his persistence. i don't know why he doesn't give up on me. He's far more patient than i deserve. Even after i bailed out of the last dinner invitation, he asked me out again. He's never deterred, it would appear. He seems almost too good to be true. Is he?

i have so many emotions swirling around in my heart and mind right now. They drain me physically and mentally. i am left with a feeling of such malaise and very little reserve energy from which to draw. i don't understand his interest in me when it would be much easier for him to go out with someone who isn't so encumbered by pain. jack's response is always, "I love you. Let me be the steadiness in your life. I will wait for you to be ready." How fortunate for me. How unfortunate for jack.

My life and jack's life have had tangled knots, but how did he rise above his circumstances seemingly unharmed and still whistling? His strength seems to be inborn. i, on the other hand, am struggling to develop strength in a fledgling fashion.

i do know that i care about jack. Do i dare say i love him? Is it risky, i wonder? i feel fortunate to simply be around his whistling. It is too bad that he has no idea of the level of comfort he provides for me. i can picture myself being with him forever, *but i can, also, picture how much it would hurt to lose him. This is the emotion for which there seems to be no cure. What did my father used to say about how to love?*

i wasn't listening then...

i'm ready to listen now...

The Loom

Olivia's father offered a sense of safety just by his presence. He was a physician on whom many people depended. To Olivia, Rachael and their younger brother, Joe, he was just the Daddy who spent much anticipated Sunday nights during their childhoods watching Lassie with them. The effects of those grueling and demanding work weeks rarely showed. He enjoyed listening to his children playfully arguing over to whom Lassie was waving as the credits rolled. Reflecting on it now, Olivia realized that his children were providing a sense of safety and love for him that he needed, perhaps, even more than they.

Their father appeared to be content. Olivia knew it was a façade. There was such a strong sense of deep-rooted sadness that permeated him and shrouded his being. He would drift off into a pensive, distant place. Olivia always thought he was too far away to reach; therefore, she never tried. She understood why he was so sad. Her brother, Charlie, had been born with a heart defect. Olivia's father adored him as they had like minds and personalities. He died at the age of three. Olivia's father rarely spoke of him. Charlie was tucked away tightly in his heart and the recesses of his mind until it was time for him to drift far, far away with his memories…

He had loved Charlie… he had lost him…

Olivia knew that there was even more to this retreat where he was a frequent guest. His only and younger sibling had drowned at the age of twelve at Girl Scout Camp when he was just sixteen. He took it upon himself to play the role of two people for his grieving parents to make up for the loss. Charlie's death only made him retreat more deeply.

He had loved his sister… he had lost her…

Olivia was two when Charlie died. She had adored him, as well. It was an indelible kind of love that is accompanied by an innocent faith that her best friend would be by her side forever and ever. They were more like joined at the hip twins, only twelve months apart. Olivia always followed his lead even if it meant wearing a gun belt. After his death, Olivia would walk around the house calling his name with an extra cookie to share. She was unable to understand why she couldn't find him. Charlie was the leader and Olivia was his shadow. Her brother and best friend had abandoned her… left her alone. It was more like cruel abandonment in an innocent child's mind. Olivia retreated.

She had loved Charlie…she had lost him.

As Olivia grew up, she found herself drifting like her father had done into that same contemplative state so far, far away. Olivia understood in only the way that souls in pain can. Her mother would practice diligently with Olivia to help her learn to speak comfortably in order to overcome her shyness. She enrolled her in ballet and piano so she could make friends and learn to be around people. She cried in ballet, but loved playing the piano. The piano became an escape. So Olivia played and played and played and let her fingers work out her shyness and build her self-confidence. The piano saved her.

By the fourth grade, a more self-reliant Olivia began to emerge. Olivia was cured in a sense, but she knew she would probably always carry the cocoon with her to make for a speedy retreat when needed. Her parents began to feel better about her, especially her father. However, he never completely let go of the feeling that he needed to continually guide her. He hurt for her as much as he had for himself. Olivia's father spent the rest of his life trying to make up for the loss of his daughter's best friend. He became her gentle protectorate and life advisor, quietly guiding her.

The doorbell rang and Olivia was forced out of her pondering thoughts. It was Jack, right on time, dependable as always. She opened the door and she thought he looked so handsome.

He looks great. i'm so excited to see him!

She successfully suppressed her thrill, as he gave her his traditional hello kiss that she loved.

i wish i could tell him how much i love that kiss.

His excited vulnerability over seeing her was always touching for Olivia.

Jack said, "You look great! I've been looking forward to seeing you. I love you!"

Me too! i just wish i could say it out loud.

Olivia was looking forward to being with him, too. She knew better than to show it.

Olivia forced these inner thoughts to the back of her mind. Jack was cooking dinner for her again at his house. She loved these nights…Jack had no idea just how much.

What was it Daddy used to tell me about loving?

i wasn't listening then…i'm ready to listen now…

Olivia's Journal

My father was the "loom", the steady foundation, for our family's life. He, also, wove warmth and strength for his friends and patients. Although he was a complex and brilliant man, he taught us through his example about how to live a more rewarding, simple kind of life. His greatest lesson was showing us how important it is to be good to the people whom you love.

My father had been concerned about me after Charlie died because i had become so withdrawn. All the photographs taken of me following Charlie's death reflected my hurt over the loss. There was seriousness in my expressions. i was always worriedly biting my lip and looking hurt and lost. Life must have seemed filled with cruel uncertainty to someone so young. How could i trust that life would ever be fair? Will i always be on the precipice of hearing sad news? Why can't life be a guarantee of tranquility-a calm, continual "picnic of pleasure"? Does god not think like that? Did god know that all i wanted was to find Charlie to give him a cookie? Did god feel bad because i never found him? Did god know he was leaving scars on a young child's heart that may never heal?

Daddy bought a doll for me after Charlie died in an effort to keep me from feeling so alone. Her name was Shrinking Violet. i can remember playing with her for hours and hours. When i pulled her string she would say, "I have butterflies in my tummy." At that point, in my young mind, Shrinking Violet was the only one who knew how it felt for me to feel lost and deserted with "butterflies in my tummy".

i loved Charlie...i lost him...

It wasn't comforting.

It wasn't peaceful.

It wasn't safe.

The Weaving

The moment that Jack laid his brown eyes on Olivia's green eyes on her first day of work at The Ragweed Garden, he knew there was an emotional intimacy-an intimacy between the two that required no spoken words. Jack knew all he needed to know just by looking through her doleful, green eyes- the windows to her soul. It was a soul that mirrored back a need for sweet, sweet caressing and attention. From that moment on, he made up his mind that he would take full responsibility to ensure that she got all the nurturing she could ever need.

Jack had never considered that the concept of love at first sight was something fathomable. It seemed so "make-believe", especially to someone who had only tasted a life of irregularity. He was even more leery of the concept of soul mates. He now knew otherwise. There was such a strong connection he felt toward Olivia that traveled beyond physical and mental. It was a feeling that took the direct route to his soul and completely usurped his heart while in the process.

Olivia's curly, auburn hair would tend to be even curlier by the end of the day from the heat and humidity. Olivia had as little control over how her hair behaved as Jack had over the deep stirrings in his heart toward her.

Olivia had a naiveté and gullibility about her that made Jack want to guide her through life by the hand making sure no one was ever mean to her. He knew better than to tell her that because it offended her. Jack knew she had spent a lifetime trying to overcome shyness and to develop her own sense of self-reliance. She had emerged as a capable woman with a deep-rooted sense of individuality.

Olivia had told Jack once that she had always felt like she was walking down the same path with everyone else only ever-so-slightly askew. Jack, however, was attracted to her comfortableness with being askew. It only made for another connection between the two. He knew he had been on that same askew path his whole life, too. But he still wanted to spend the rest of his life making sure that no one was ever mean to Olivia.

There was a dichotomy of simplicity and complexity about Olivia upon which Jack couldn't quite put his finger. Her mystique piqued his interest. She would become so absorbed in her work that Jack got the feeling she wasn't even aware anyone else was around. She would drift pensively… out of range… Jack longed to know the secret to penetrating her fractious, protective layer.

Jack couldn't identify with Olivia's losses, because he didn't know what it even felt like to have a father or a brother or a sister. He had, however, spent a large portion of his life in that hotel room conjuring up wonderful images of what a real family might have been like. He created the perfect family in his mind, and stored it away to be drawn upon whenever necessary.

Fortunately, Jack was able to have a taste throughout high school of one real family. There was a generous family who practically adopted him, allowing him free servings of a normal existence whenever he needed them. Jack was allowed to come and go at his leisure. It was, actually, the words from one of his "adoptive" mothers that had made the most lasting imprint on his life. She had said, "Jack, to be happy, act happy and soon you will be." They were words that Jack allowed to run continuously through his mind from that day forward.

That was the turning point in his life when Jack began to whistle, and whistle, and whistle…

And so Jack *WAS* happy.

Olivia's mother knew that something was wrong when her husband began coming home from work with notes in his pockets. They were descriptions of friends, co-workers and patients. He would sort through once familiar names and Olivia's mother would help recreate their histories. Even sadder, most of them were people who had been his favorite patients and friends. It was unfortunate that some of the people he no longer recognized had once meant a great deal to him.

His family soon began to notice that he was developing a compulsive nature. He became obsessed with taking out the trash and the way the cars were parked in the driveway. He was fifty-six years old and looked healthy. It was, however, a deceiving camouflage to hide the insidious disease that was slowly robbing his once brilliant, kind mind.

The day Olivia's father's condition was diagnosed as early onset Alzheimer's, he resigned from his position at the hospital. Following in his usual, thorough style, he became a most industrious Alzheimer's patient. He worked diligently at menial tasks around the house, filling his days walking the dogs, doing the dishes and the wash. He established himself as the best neighborhood paperboy. Vacationing neighbors and the elderly counted on him to pick up their newspapers and put them on their porches. Her father's simplistic routines filled up his idle time for him, but he managed it courageously without complaint. Sadly, his new routines were a far cry from the intensity of his work during his medical career.

Olivia's father was thrown into an unnatural state that no one could have predicted. His world was slowly becoming an abnormal, alien world of confusion. It was the same frightening world that he had once made feel so safe for Olivia. She knew her safe and sound world would slowly be disappearing right along with her father's mind... as it silently... painfully... slipped away...

It's too late to listen now...

He walked wherever he went in his small town. At first, the family was concerned for his safety until they realized that his friends and the patients he had once taken care of were now watching out for their beloved friend. After a nine year illness, he died leaving behind a shining example of valiancy.

"You and the children have been my whole life. I want to say this one last time that I am grateful to you and what you have been to me. If I could live my whole life again, I wouldn't change a thing. How fortunate I have been. Please remind the children every now and then that their Daddy loves them more than they can ever know. I leave you my love...all of it...forever."

These were her father's loving words in a sealed letter he had written to Olivia's mother twenty years before to be read at the event of his death. The words were etched in Olivia's memory for posterity. Her father could shell out a sense of comfort and calmness just by his mere presence. He was still doing it posthumously through the written word. He had a way of making people feel safe in his protective hands. The feeling of safety was what Olivia knew she would miss the most.

Will i ever be able to feel safe again?

Mustering up heaping portions of courage, Olivia decided it was time to sift through the manila envelopes that were labeled just "Daddy". It was perplexingly sad how the essence of his sixty-four years was packed into only a few envelopes. They were filled with some of her father's favorite quotes written in his distinctive handwriting. It always gave Olivia a jolt to see her father's handwriting. There was something so sad and strange about it for her. It was proof that he had existed as a real, living, breathing person with thoughts that were uniquely his and his own personal style of handwriting.

Olivia remembered receiving letters from her father while she was at summer camp. Sticking to true, physician style his handwriting was difficult to read. She had to get her camp counselors, who were more adept at deciphering than she was, to read his letters for her. Now...he would never write again. It gave her such a strange feeling.

In a hurried cram session, Olivia's mind raced to recall the essence of her father and his wisdom. In the whirlwind of emotions, the best she could recall were little remnants of advice he had given such as, "Give good strong handshakes, be nice to people, and do what feels right in your heart." Surely, there was far more to her father than three statements.

If i could have just one more conversation with him, i promise i'd listen much better now.

Olivia wondered why it is typically in death that beautiful adjectives are used to describe people. These are words that the loved ones who have died needed to know while they were alive to hear them. She thought what a disservice it is at this ineffective late date when your loved one is out of physical hearing range.

Olivia's father was an introspective and humble man who would much rather have been the observer than the attention seeker in spite of a lifetime of accomplishments.

Olivia remembered that her father used to always say, "When I die, I don't want any fuss. Just come down to breakfast and say, "Things sure are different without Daddy today." That's why this unassuming man was buried in a plain and simple pine coffin that he would have no doubt picked. No fuss, no extravagances…just simple simplicity. Things sure were definitely different without her Daddy…and not just at breakfast.

It wasn't until the mountain of letters came in following her father's death that Olivia truly began to understand what an exceptional man he was. Judging by his humble nature, she was sure he had not been aware of it himself. He had been known to his patients for his listening skills and advising abilities for a resolution of their woes. It made him even more special in her mind.

Olivia never knew that her father graduated Phi Beta Kappa from college in three years and was ranked near the top of his medical school class. She was stunned that her father had never mentioned any of his achievements.

Olivia learned that many times, while he was in general practice, he would personally pick up women in labor at their homes and take them to the hospital. According to the letters from his grateful patients, many times he accepted vegetables for payment. His salt-of-the-earth patients with their unpretentious ways were the ones who meant the most to him.

Olivia's father felt such an empathy toward his patients while he was in general practice that billing them was difficult for him. He knew that many of them did not have enough money to pay for his services. It weighed on his conscience. He decided that he would rather be a hospital employee where it wouldn't be necessary for him to bill his patients.

In addition, her father's sponge-like mind was continually searching for more ways to challenge it. He was intrigued by the human anatomy and fascinated by the science behind it. Olivia was in the third grade when her father decided to return to medical school to specialize in pathology. His need for more knowledge was quenched and his conscience was at peace. He used to say that "the autopsy table was the great equalizer."

Olivia's father volunteered his services in Vietnam working as a physician in a hospital. He once said that the "Orientals are different from Americans, but they cry the same tears when they lose a loved one." After his death, Olivia's mother found the journal he had kept while he was in Vietnam. One of the entries after a hard, yet gratifying day was, "I'm hot.

I'm windblown. I'm dirty. Boy, do I feel good!" He summed up the essence of his own nature with these simple sentences. He was a quiet goodwill ambassador to many people who valued his simple, generous ways.

One of the letters from a former patient said, "Your Daddy meant so much to my family. I remember when he made a house call when my son was sick. He calmed me down by saying in the most comforting way, "He's sick right now, but he's going to get well."

Another letter was from a woman who had a mental breakdown following a difficult time in her life. She said, "God only knows what your Daddy meant to me. He was so caring, so understanding, helping in ways that I can remember to this day." Reading the letters only made Olivia's desire stronger to once again feel the safety and security her Daddy's mere presence offered to her.

The family found receipts indicating that he had anonymously sent money to send disadvantaged children to camp. They, also, discovered letters that he had written to high school graduates encouraging them to believe in themselves. The more refreshing aspect was that he never required credit for his good deeds. It was a life lesson in true goodness. Olivia knew that it was far too late to express interest in her father's work, travels, good deeds and his deepest thoughts at this point.

i wasn't listening then... i'm ready to listen now...

Olivia's Journal

i remember throughout my father's illness, my mother would take him on long, long drives in the country to keep him content. When he would see a license tag from another state, he would say in a childlike way, "Boy, they sure are far from home." I think about that statement often in comparison to how his illness left me feeling. The disease not only stole his mind, it stole my sense of safety that only a Daddy can provide. It left me feeling "a long way from home" and its security.

Throughout his illness, i always asked, "Why?" My mother asked, "Why not?" And she accepted it. She seems to have an inner strength that allows her to have this kind of attitude. i am not that strong. i'll just have to listen, observe and drink in every ounce of fortitude she can throw my way. i'm thirsty for it.

i have always felt so guilty that i chose to leave the hospital when my father was taken off the ventilator and his death was imminent. i was the only family member who "ran away". i ran because i loved him too much to watch him die, not because i didn't love him. Hopefully, he understood.

i think he would...i hope...

It took my father's death for me to realize that simple is better. It is far more enriching to live your life uncluttered by frivolous extravagances. i put all of my jewelry in the safe after Daddy died, and i have not been interested in "adorning"

*myself with a single piece since then.
Things don't have value. People do. That is
the message my father spent his life trying
to get across to us. Why did it have to take
his death for me to lock away such
trivialities with no real value? i am left
with a safe bearing a few beautiful,
meaningless pieces of jewelry, when all
along the true gem was in the form of my
father...and he is gone...*

*My father used to say to Rachael and
me, "You girls look mighty pretty today."
What i would give to hear that sentence
once more. i know i would respond
differently with an appropriate thank you
instead of barely acknowledging his kind
words. Daddy would always say to us no*

matter how small the accomplishment, "I'm
so proud of you!" i would love to have the
chance to tell him that we were the ones
who were proud of him.

He had a way of gently guiding
Rachael, Joe and me. i can remember being
an inexperienced driver of fifteen with my
learner's permit. i was in need of guidance
and a shot of confidence. My father asked
me to drive him to the mountains one
afternoon. He sat completely relaxed the
whole way up the mountain, as if he felt
perfectly safe in my unsure hands. i would
guess that god wants me to feel safe in his
hands. But god's hands don't feel safe to me
right now. i am as unsure in his hands as

when i was fifteen and driving around the dangerous curves. i want to feel safe again.

i loved my father...i have lost him...

i read a quote today by Charles Lindbergh that said, "It isn't the moment that you are struck that you need courage, but for the long uphill climb back to sanity, faith, and security." Maybe if i could get my faith back then there would be some hope for security.

While i was looking outside the kitchen window today washing dishes at the kitchen sink, i happened to notice a mourning dove sitting on the birdbath. i could have sworn he looked straight at me. i felt a lift that carried me through the day.

i just wish i could feel that god was by my side as well.

i tried to pray again today. No luck.

i loved god... i lost god...

Now that Daddy is gone, i'm afraid i will never be able to remember what he told me about how to love.

i wasn't listening then...

i'm ready to listen now...

The Double Knots

The doctors say Rachael has a fifty-fifty chance for survival," Olivia's mother said. Total numbness and shock swept over Olivia's body. 'How could that be possible? Olivia thought. She was perfectly fine a few days ago. How could it be? I saw her laughing just yesterday.'

Words are so powerful. Shocking words are even more potent. It felt like a sneak attack with no warning. The next paralyzing words were, "They are putting her on life support. Even if she survives, she will have brain damage." The brutal ambush left Olivia feeling pummeled by unfairness.

Rachael was on life support for two weeks. The next call came from Olivia's brother, saying "They are taking her off life support today. She will die soon."

How do you prepare for a moment like that?

You don't.

Olivia walked through the funeral process as if she were walking around in a dream. She greeted, she hugged, she cried. She wanted everyone to go away and she wanted everyone to stay. It felt like an unnatural state. When Olivia spotted the hearse with her sister in it in the church parking lot the reality and finality of it hit her in one swift glance. She glanced away even more swiftly as if to make the whole terrible scene disappear. But it didn't work.

If god was supposed to be so good, then why didn't he heal

Charlie, Daddy, and Rachael when it was requested by all of us

through prayer?

Throughout the greeting process at the funeral, Olivia kept overhearing people saying to her mother, "You have had so much sadness in your life." Her mother's response every time was, "Well, I don't see it that way. I've had a lot of good, too." Olivia wondered to herself how her mother could have such steady faithfulness in the midst of unsteady strife.

Olivia had discussed with her mother that it seemed so unfair that they had had so much loss in their lives. Her mother simply replied, "Why not us? Would you have preferred that it have happened to your best friend? In life, we have to accept the semi-bad and the horrendous both spread with ample amounts of good."

i still say, "Why?" i cannot accept this. god needs to answer my questions.

So Olivia's mother accepted adversity once again and the harsh reality of life's uncertainty.

Olivia's thoughts turned toward her brother, Joe. He had been unable to attend Rachael's funeral because of his long- term health issues.

Rachael had been so concerned about Joe's health right before she died. They loved each other so much. i know Joe wishes he could have attended her funeral, but i know Rachael would have understood.

He had once been an avid hunter and fisherman and was adept at both. He longed to be able to work a full, hard day once again.

With constant optimistic spirits and a sense of complacency, he is able to visualize healthiness as a viable possibility for himself again. Olivia knew that this attitude descended directly from their mother and her example.

Olivia thought back on the night that Rachael died. It was difficult to concentrate on it for very long. It felt as if she only had enough strength to think about it for small increments at a time. The reality of it was far too overwhelming for her mind to comprehend.

Olivia's mother told her about an experience she had at the hospital while Rachael was on the ventilator. The intensive care ward becomes the common denominator of emotions, where suffering families come together. They become your world and you become theirs.

While Rachael was struggling to remain with her family, there was one large, but very close-knit family waiting in the same room. The two grieving families answered each other's frantic calls from worried loved ones and friends. They shared stories of their special loved ones. The other family had gathered in joyous anticipation for the birth of a beloved family member's fifth son. The mood suddenly turned downward when she suffered a cardiac arrest, and she was hanging on to life by a thread. A paradox of dual emotions of happiness and sadness overcame them.

Rachael and this lady became roommates in the intensive care ward with each being kept alive by awkward machines. They were separated by a thin curtain and unaware of each other's presence. The commonality, however, was that they were both desperately loved by families only a few feet away. They were praying and hoping that their loved ones would be healed.

The phone in the waiting room kept ringing for the lady's son. He was a high school senior athlete being pursued by professional basketball coaches who were each fighting to lure him to their team. Olivia's mother talked and cried with him often during that long arduous week. After several phone interruptions he turned to her mother and said, "I don't know what to do. The only thing my mother has ever wanted me to do is to go to college."

After Rachael died, Olivia's mother was stepping on the hospital elevator for the last time to begin the grim task of funeral arrangements. She heard footsteps hurriedly approaching just before the doors were ready to close. The boy's long, strong arm came thrusting into the elevator and grabbed her hand. As he quickly expressed how sorry he was for their loss, the doors began to close. Olivia's mother squeezed his hand as she gave a quick, but poignant, instruction to him, "Go to college," she said as the doors closed. And so ended their brief, but memorable and tragic journey.

The day of Rachael's death had potential for heartache and tears. Instead, it became a day of fellowship of which Rachael would have approved. Olivia's college friends came from all areas of the state to spend the night with her. It turned into a pajama party of love. She knew Rachael would have enjoyed being a part of it. Somehow, Olivia had a strong sense that she was, in fact, among them with her trademark laugh.

Olivia missed Rachael so much that whole night and every day and night and every breathing moment since that day. Most of all, she missed watching the way her right nostril quivered when she was caught up in a funny moment as she laughed that infectious laugh.

i wish i had told her how much i loved her laugh.

One friend drove up after painting a room in her house. Olivia noticed the bottom of her feet were white. She asked, "What is that on the bottom of your feet?" Her friend's reply was, "It's paint. When I heard about Rachael, I put the paintbrush down, picked up my keys and drove straight here." Olivia realized how lucky she was to have "Drop-everything-and-go" friends. She had vivid memories of Rachael having been a dedicated "Drop-everything- and-go" sister, too.

Does god know what that meant to me?

Olivia had always loved to write. She loved words. She loved the expression of thoughts becoming beautiful sentences. Olivia never anticipated that the words she loved would be used to write her own sister's obituary. She, however, agreed to take on the bittersweet task. How could she compile her sister's enriching life into one small column? It seemed like a daunting and overwhelming task. There was one bizarre moment when Olivia had a question she needed to clear up about Rachael for accuracy purposes. As she was reaching for the phone to make the call, the harsh reality struck. Numbness took over once again.

It's hard to believe that i won't see my wonderful sister again in my lifetime. i will miss her every single day. Does god know that? Does god care? Is god listening?

Olivia did manage to write through the foggy haze of it all. She wrote:

Rachael was a rare and special person and you knew it when you were in her presence. She had a multitude of friends and an ability to extend herself to others. She took great care in the nurturing of her friendships. Rachael not only had beautiful porcelain skin on the outside, but a rare and precious porcelain heart as well. Rachael radiated kindness, intelligence and great wit. She had a wonderful sense of humor and an infectious laugh. Her friends were naturally drawn back for more helpings of

Rachael's great company. In lieu of flowers, love your family and cherish every moment.

Olivia's Journal

It is interesting to me to watch the world continuing on as if nothing has happened. Don't people know that the world has come to a screeching halt? The sun is still coming up, birds are singing, people still go out to get the morning paper and school buses are running on schedule. How can life keep moving along at its normal pace while i'm frozen and floundering in numb suspension?

i loved Rachael... i have lost her...

It is the Christmas season now. It is not joyous or jolly in the least for me. How can there be delightful anticipation when all i am aware of is that i will never be able to celebrate a special occasion with Rachael ever again? i can't stand the idea of not seeing her name on my Christmas list with ideas for unique gifts especially for her. She always put such thought and effort into the gifts she bought for all of us. She spent way too much money. We knew that it gave her pleasure to watch us all be happy and she would go to great lengths to do it.

We will miss Rachael so much. Does god know that, i wonder? Does god care? Is god listening?

Why didn't god heal such a wonderful person like we asked in prayer?

i went to a Christmas party last night. i had on a great looking festive, red sweater. i wanted so much to fit in with everyone. i thought if i could look the part, maybe I could be a part of the gaiety. The moment i walked in the door and saw everyone laughing and having fun, i quickly began plotting my escape. i looped through the back den, around by the kitchen and back out the front door. How could i pretend to be happy when my heart was so full of tears? Will i ever be able to walk around in the same dimension with everyone else again?

i've done a small amount of Christmas shopping, but my heart isn't in it. It seems so petty... "things" seem so petty and unnecessary. i just want to laugh with my sister again. That would be un-petty and necessary.

Rachael was so funny. She could impersonate anyone and kept us laughing with her antics for hours. If i could just laugh again...a real laugh...not a fake one. Does god know i want to laugh again, i wonder?

i will never forget the outpouring from friends and family who became a kind of balm to make the unbearable pain bearable. A good friend lives behind me and it gives me comfort to see his light on at night as evidence that he is there. i had told him about the comfort it gives me. The day i got in from Rachael's funeral he had left a message saying, "I'm going to leave the light on all night for you so you'll know I'm here, if you need anything." He called me later saying, "I didn't know Rachael, but I want to come to your house one day. I want to know all about her." i believe they were the kindest and most insightful words i had heard. He made the world feel just a little bit all right for me. When we talk he always says, "Tell me a Rachael story." His touching words were perfect for helping to take the edge off the pain of my days that felt anything but perfect.

Sometimes i think that people are afraid to broach a subject they think might be painful or uncomfortable for a person who is grieving. But i appreciate when it is acknowledged that my sister was a real, breathing person with integrity and worth. Rachael was an exceptional person. It makes it even more difficult to accept that such a viable person is gone.

i remember Rachael would always go to see the same movies three and four times with different sets of friends. She would justify it by saying she loved to go just to watch her friends enjoy a movie that she knew was good. Rachael was the definition of what it means to be an unselfish friend.

i had a friend who perceptively greeted me with a simple question that got straight to the bottom line of grief. She said, "Don't you miss your sister so much?" i thought she worded it perfectly. My answer to this question will forever be a resounding, "YES!" Enough said. That was the end of our short, but meaningful conversation.

She is right. i will miss Rachael every moment of every day for the rest of my life...

Why is it that the only image i can see when i'm trying to fall asleep is the way Rachael laughed. i loved the way her right nostril quivered every time she laughed especially hard. i always thought it was so cute. i don't recall ever telling her that. Why didn't i tell her when i had the chance?

i am trying to be strong, but i feel I am drowning in these sad circumstances. There are days when i would like to allow myself to just be weak. i think it would be okay temporarily. i just don't want to let my friends down. They want me to move quickly through this process and be myself again. i certainly understand why, but I need them to allow me to be weak ...just for a little while.

i not only lost my sister, but three darling, little children lost their Mom. Her son innocently asked if his Mom was going to be home for Christmas or if, perhaps, a magician could bring her back? How do you explain loss to a precious child? Why did god leave us with the difficult task of explaining loss to an innocent child? What a dilemma god put in our laps.

i returned to church today out of a sense of obligation rather than desire. i found myself listening absentmindedly. i did, however, listen carefully to the hymn,

O Love That Wilt Not Let Me Go. i could identify with some of the phrases such as "flickering torch" and "weary soul". Those phrases so accurately describe how i'm feeling. There was one stanza that will take further exploration on my part to believe. The contemplative verse was:

O Joy that seekest me through pain,

I cannot close my heart to thee.

I trace the rainbow through the rain.

And feel the promise is not vain,

That morn shall tearless be.

My view:

i have closed my heart and i can't seem to find the rainbow in the rain. i do feel the promise is in vain and that i suspect i will not have a morning that is not filled with tears for some time to come.

i find myself going to bed as early as possible to block out the pain that i feel so strongly during the day. There is such a sense of malaise and a lack of energy. This does not feel healthy to me. Therefore, i have decided to implement a plan for survival. It will be a plan to get my energy back, so i can feel a part of the world again. There must be order to the plan.

My Plan for Grief Survival:
1) When i wake up each morning, let my first thought be, 'How would my father and Rachael want me to behave today?'

They would want me to be happy and productive.

2) Surround myself with friends who make me feel good and who make me laugh. Go out to lunch with these happy friends two or three times per week. They will be my lifelines.

3) Break down my day into manageable segments, so it will not feel too demanding. Do this by making a list every night of the things i wish to accomplish in a day. Never make the list too long, so the day does not feel overwhelming. Never make it too short, so it will feel like a productive

day. Think in terms of one day at a time, one moment at a time and just making it through as happily as possible.

4) Don't act like i feel "put upon" or feel sorry for myself. It is very unattractive. i am not the only one with troubles. Keep in mind that there are a good many wonderful aspects of my life....my friends, my work, jack, and my good memories.

5) Take fast-paced long walks. It will be mental therapy. Walk with friends, too. Keep the conversation light and positive. Avoid discussing heavy issues.

6) *Get beyond myself.   Think of someone who has a need and act on it. Send a card. Cook a meal for a friend in need. Stay in touch with friends. This is imperative.*

7) *Understand that this is a lengthy process and will be accomplished by taking baby steps.*

8) *Smile a lot and soon my heart will be smiling as well, like Jack.*

9) *Participate actively in a Bible Study program at my church with an open*

mind. Make this hour in the week a priority. Maybe god will become real.

10) Journal. Express my feelings through my writing. i can look back later and have a gauge for my progress.

11) Learn from the knots and use them as a vehicle to become more highly evolved as a person. Embrace the silver and gold aspects. Use them as a pathway to ultimate happiness.

12) Move forward...keep moving forward for myself, my family and my lost loved ones...

13) i am not going to be Scarlet and think about starting this plan tomorrow. It will be implemented today!

At least in the midst of the pain and confusion, i do have jack who is steadfast and so kind to me. i don't want anything that feels complicated at this point. i don't have the energy for complexity. i am so content to just sit beside him. It is a simplistic escape from a world that is too real and too unreal all at the same time. jack seems to be able to just let me be without comment or suggestions on how i should be feeling. i appreciate it so, but i just can't seem to form the words to tell him how much.

This is a personal and lonely journey that i have to work out on my own. And i will. It will take a great deal of time for resolution, i suspect. How can you be expected to have a cut-off point for grieving when you have lived and laughed for several decades with family whom you loved so dearly? i will work through this, but it has to be on my own time. i hope that my friends will be patient and supportive through this complicated process of grief. It will be invaluable to me in the long run. This i know for sure.

When i went for my walk this morning, i saw a mourning dove sitting on the telephone wires. It brought tears to my eyes to see my familiar "guardian". It's interesting how a simple, fragile bird can offer me such a dose of strength. i will embrace anything that provides a semblance of comfort. For just a moment, i did not feel alone.

The Silver Threads

“Hey, Olivia, Do you feel like lunch again today?” said the familiar voice of her good friend and confidante, Liz. Olivia's first retreating thought was to say no. Liz detected the hesitancy to which she was accustomed from her friend.

She said, “Olivia, remember your plan of going out to lunch with your friends. I'm making you stick to it. I'll be there to pick you up shortly. Be ready.”

As Olivia was hanging up the phone, she could feel her heart smiling. Liz had been a steadfast and loyal friend to her through the hills and the valleys. All of her friends had sensed Olivia's sadness. They were loyally ushering her back to a semblance of normality again.

After they were seated at their favorite lunch hang-out, Liz said, "Tell me a funny Rachael story!" Olivia was touched by her friend's insight, as she began the process of sorting through which one of the many funny stories to tell.

Although Rachael was known for her keen intelligence, it seemed that she was always in some kind of dire, but funny, dilemma. Olivia's mind was flooded with hilarious thoughts as she conjured up memories that made her smile just at the reflection. Rachael seemed to inevitably find herself in messes that only became fodder for future entertainment and laughs...such as now. Rachael entertained her friends with countless hours of stories and flawless, hysterical impersonations.

Olivia's mother said that as a child, Rachael was always the one who had to be watched so carefully because she could disappear in seconds flat. Her inquiring mind led her on exploring expeditions to quench her thirst for knowledge. As she grew into adulthood, she continued to have this same compelling desire to see and feel all aspects of a world she found to be wonderfully enriching and exciting.

In addition, Rachael would suffer some physical blemish prior to special events in her life. On her first day of high school, she arrived swollen and red-faced with a bad case of poison ivy covering her face. It only naturally followed that upon her first day at college she had a severe case of sun-poisoning with her face swollen twice its size. Camps were a disaster for her as well. Her parents always knew to expect a phone call requesting them to pick her up, so she could heal from her injuries. The list ran from broken arms, eye injuries to scraping the bottom of the pool. One of her camp catastrophes was a bumpy ride on a runaway horse. Her tenacity, however, overruled her head, and she always returned for more doses of daring adventures.

Rachael was once on a church retreat. Knowing she should stay away from horses because of her past experiences, she therefore, sensibly, chose a pony. As she was trotting along on the side of the mountain, the pony stopped short, and Rachael went flying over her head and she slid on her face through a field of freshly mowed hay. The sharp points scraped her entire face. True to form she was due to have her homecoming attendant's picture made by a professional photographer two days later. Her slide on the side of the mountain was captured for posterity, resulting in year's worth of laughter. Rachael was always laughing the hardest at her own expense. Naturally, her nostril would be quivering in that distinct, cute way it had when she was particularly tickled.

Funny things continued to follow her through her career. Olivia recalled the day Rachael called her laughing about having fallen in an air-conditioning vent at work. She was hurrying into the bathroom forgetting that construction workers had removed the vent. One leg was so wedged in the vent that she was immobile. Her skirt was billowing all around her as she waited to be rescued while lodged in the floor.

Liz jolted Rachael out of her mind's scrapbook of funny Rachael moments saying, "Well, which one are you going to tell me?" Holding off a burst of laughter, Olivia said, "Let me tell you the one about the night Rachael and Josh met for their blind date. Josh had told her that he would be wearing a green and white striped shirt. Rachael walked in assuming that his distinct shirt would be evident and Josh could be found quite easily. She walked into the restaurant to find that all the restaurant employees had on green and white striped shirts as their work attire. Rachael timidly sat for awhile wondering if they would connect. Josh was already there and had observed the dilemma as well. He got up the courage to take a stab that she might be Rachael. That first date began in reels of laughter and the laughter never stopped through their dating years and ten years of a beautiful marriage."

Josh and Rachael were comforted.

Josh and Rachael were peaceful.

Josh and Rachael were safe.

Josh and Rachael were each other's homes. She was sure that they loved in the way her father had advised.

What was it that Daddy used to say about how to love?

i wasn't listening then... i'm ready to listen now...

Olivia's Journal

There is such beauty in warehousing a lifetime of memories that can be revisited and brought to the forefront at any given moment. Gratefully, i know the value of good friends and in having a sense of humor. i never completely realized until now that they are the lifeline that balances grief. i think people feel it may be disrespectful to continue laughing about circumstances surrounding our loved ones we have lost. i miss them with an eternal "soul-ache". However, it is essential for the healing process to laugh. i know for certain that my father and Rachael would rather that i be laughing than crying.

i can remember through my father's illness, as his mind became more and more childlike, he would do things that resulted in that healing kind of laughter for us. i don't think he would have minded that we smiled over him.

i remember that one rainy Easter morning we had resorted to hiding the eggs in the house for the grandchildren's annual Easter egg hunt. Daddy, at this point, in his illness had a compulsive sense of order. Eggs everywhere upset that order. So while we were cleaning the kitchen before the big hunt, Daddy took it upon himself to go on his own personal egg hunt to restore order in the household. The children came in to hunt for the Easter eggs and there wasn't one egg to be found anywhere.

We smiled. We laughed.

Somehow we knew he would have been laughing, too. And that makes it okay. Laughter and comic relief are imperative for healing. i know this for sure.

The Gold Threads

"Hey Aunt Olivia! We can't wait to spend the weekend at your house!" said Annie. She was Rachael's eight year old and the leader of the pack of three.

The precious, sweet voice on the other end of the phone touched Olivia's heart to its very core.

Olivia replied, "I can't wait to see you all, too! I have fun things planned for us to do!"

Rachael's three children were the highlights in the midst of the tragedy of their Mom's death. Fortunately, Rachael had meticulously made a wonderful choice in choosing her husband. Olivia's family knew that her children would be well-fathered and well-mothered by him. Olivia was thinking about how they had shared such a rare connection and an unsurpassed devotion to each other.

Rachael had spent ten years broadening her mind and expanding her knowledge of the world by traveling. She always kept an eye out for the perfect man in her travels. She was complacent as she waited. Her patience truly paid off when she and Josh met on that blind date arranged through a mutual friend. Interestingly, Rachael had traveled the world and all the while Josh was right under her nose in the same town and a member of the same large urban church. They married several years later. Their three children, Annie, Will, and Kathleen followed in rapid succession. Rachael and Josh were as devoted to their children as they were to each other.

Olivia forced these thoughts to the back of her mind for the time being. She needed to put her energy towards planning a fun weekend for Rachael's children. She began by stopping off at the local appliance shop to pick up the biggest discarded refrigerator box she could find. She made another stop for paints, brushes and glitter. Olivia found herself being caught up in the fun and looking forward to their arrival. The children spent the whole weekend transforming that ugly cardboard box into The Groovy House. It was painted, glittered and sponged in the midst of laughs and giggles. They crawled in and out pretending it had many different purposes to suit their fantasies. It was exactly what Olivia had in mind.

It seems so unfair that i am the one enjoying Rachael's

children when she should be here with us.

The rest of the weekend was spent making and decorating cookies. They crawled up in bed together and watched movies and read stories. Somehow, the cookie crumbs falling all around the house and the paint stains on the rug were a small price to pay for the great return of watching Rachael's children having fun and laughing. Olivia sensed that Rachael was there among them with her gentle, smiling spirit.

Olivia's Journal

i had the best time this weekend with Rachael's children. At first, it was painful to be around them because i was guilt-ridden that i was the one being able to hear their laughter...and Rachael was not. There was such a sense of unjustness.

i so look forward to many more fun times. i am on such a difficult and complicated journey right now. It is hard to reach out until my cup can refill. i yearn for this time. It will come. i know it will. i am comforted that the three of them have each other and they are developing under Josh's steadfast guidance. He knows how to create the balance with helping them remember their Mom and yet

allowing them to move forward in a
healthy fashion, too.

i can visualize myself at Will's sporting
events and shopping with Annie and
Kathleen for their prom and wedding
dresses as we share girl confidences and
just do girl stuff. i must hurry and heal, so
i can create memories with them for their
sakes and Rachael's sake.

i do need to have a clear perception of
why god didn't answer our prayers to heal
such a wonderful person. One thing that i
know for sure is that i no longer feel sorry
for myself. i am more aware of all the good
in my life. This is a good sign. i remind
myself often of Anne Frank's quote, "I don't
think of all the misery, but of all the

beauty that still remains." i see the good. It is possible to grow as a person from tragedy, if you allow yourself. i am still, however, disillusioned with god. i'm continually searching for understanding. Why didn't he answer our prayers to heal Rachael? And so the journey continues...

Rachael's children are the "highlights" in the whole tragedy. In addition, i had another highlight over the weekend. When i went outside to bring The Groovy House inside, i noticed a mourning dove sitting in the birdbath. Somehow, i sensed that this observant dove had witnessed a weekend of fertilization of the body and soul.

i'm glad i was able to have this weekend of fun with the children. i had been *carrying some guilt after Rachael's death. It helped relieve my conscience a bit. Rachael had asked me to baby sit for her children one night so that she and her husband could go to the movies. i felt so guilty that i begged off with an excuse. How was i supposed to know she was going to die two months later? i wish i had said yes. It has plagued me every day since her death.*

Fortunately, a friend of mine helped me with my guilt. She said, "You can't fault yourself for occasional times, when you can't grant requests. Look at the big picture of your whole life with Rachael. Was this behavior a pattern or was it an exception?

If it's an exception, then you should wipe away all your guilt."

It was an exception. My guilt was cured.

i just wish i could remember what it was my father used to say about how to love.

> *i wasn't listening then...*
> *i'm ready to listen now...*

The Golden Tassel

Olivia woke up with that same old feeling of malaise. Sunday had come around again with its great regularity. She tossed around the idea of sleeping in and having a lazy morning. Something nagged at her though, and she found herself in her closet trying to select the proper matching ensemble for church. How could she have known that she was dressing for a monumental, pivotal moment that would cure her aching heart? Confusion and inner turmoil were about to become emotions of the past for her.

Olivia knew she was late when she heard the final bells ringing indicating that the choir was getting into place. Little did she know that the most important church service of her entire life was about to begin, as she slid into the back pew. She quickly sent up a semblance of a prayer as she knelt. Then she settled into her typical, half-hearted lukewarm listening state of mind. The minister had a kind and humble nature combined with a sharp mind. She could reach deeply into the hearts of the congregation with her calm style of delivery. In spite of this, Olivia didn't know how even this minister could impart enough wisdom to aid her searching, aching mind and heart. The search party in Olivia's heart had given up hope months ago of finding a peaceful resolution, as she wavered on the precipice between doubt and faith. Olivia drifted a bit while thinking of her grocery list for the coming week.

Olivia, however, felt herself beginning to take notice when the minister started her incantation to God. She thought it was a particularly beautiful plea. It was to a God who felt more like a long, lost friend -- a friend who was on sabbatical away from Olivia's heart. He had left her with "butterflies in her tummy" to flounder alone. The minister simply stated, "Lord, in your infinite wisdom move me out of the way with all my sins, shortcomings and failings. May I stand behind the cross so that the good news of thy Son will shine through".

Good news? There's good news?

She had Olivia's full attention as she started her sermon. She began telling a story-an all too familiar story of a boy who had been on a ventilator following an accident. Powerful prayer chains had circulated with a vengeance instigated by the boy's family, friends and even strangers. It was Olivia's sister's exact scenario. His mother was so certain that the prayers would be answered for him to be healed. She had lived a lifetime of faith and obedience to God. She continued to be optimistic that God would heal her son even after they decided to disconnect him from life support. The boy died and the woman was thrown into a state of confusion about her faith and had anger towards God. The lady went to her minister for guidance and help in understanding why God had not healed her beloved son. He had obviously chosen to ignore all the prayers. The minister said, "Let's look up the definition of healing." They discovered that in Greek the word to "heal" does not mean to cure. It means, "to make whole".

To heal means TO MAKE WHOLE.
To heal means TO MAKE WHOLE.

The floodgate to Olivia's closed off subconscious and conscious mind opened unexpectedly. A soothing peacefulness settled all around Olivia.

The prayers WERE ANSWERED!
The prayers WERE ANSWERED!

Olivia sat there in a shocked, but tranquil silence as she absorbed the profoundness.

Rachael WAS healed!
Rachael WAS healed!

Rachael's mind and body were made "whole" after all...not in an earthly form, but in an even more beautiful and more whole heavenly form.

Charlie's heart was healed, TOO!
Daddy's mind was healed, TOO!

As Olivia was accepting this first revelation, the minister offered another powerful insight for her. She said that even when you have stopped believing in prayer, finding it pointless, that's when the Holy Spirit steps in and prays for you. A cry of pain and anguish is a form of a prayer, too.

The Holy Spirit was praying for ME.
The Holy Spirit was praying for ME.

Feeling overcome from too many years of internalized emotion, Olivia knew she had to make a fast getaway. She glanced upward briefly and saw a painting of the most humble looking Jesus in his simple robed attire. He had a gentle expression on his face and his hands were reaching out. She noticed the painting every Sunday, but this was the first time Olivia felt he was reaching outward just to her this day, this very moment, as if to say, "I've been here all along. I was listening." She had chosen to ignore the gift of open arms in exchange for tackling the cruel world alone. She was finally ready to reach back at long last with a heart full of love instead of tears.

There IS a rainbow through the rain!

Olivia clutched her Bible to her chest as she slid out of the pew to escape from something so powerful. A piece of paper fell out of it onto the floor. She bent over to pick it up and swiftly exited out the side door. Olivia knew that for the first time she was not fearfully running away. She was, instead, running towards the sanctity of safety and freedom.

Olivia sat in her car and cried years of tears of pain and joy. The open wound in her heart was now filled with a tranquil comprehension of spiritual love. Olivia was listening now.

The butterlies in my tummy are finally gone.

When Olivia arrived home, she realized she was still clutching the paper that had fallen on the church floor. She looked down and noticed that it was a note in her father's signature handwriting.

The note was written in bold letters with an even bolder message saying:

Dear Olivia,

When you find an enduring love that is real, love passionately, love completely, love fearlessly, as if tomorrow is not a remote possibility. Treasure every millisecond derived from the joy of loving and of being loved. It is the greatest gift you can give yourself and the one you love. The great return is that your heart and soul are nourished, however fleetingly. It is far more rewarding than not loving at all.

With Enduring Love,
Daddy

Olivia stood staring at her father's poignant words she had been trying to recall for so long. She thought to herself, 'My Father and my father are guiding me still.' Amazing.

Olivia could feel herself stepping out of the cocoon that had sheltered her since Charlie's death so many years ago.

I am free to love God.
I am free to love Jack.
Jack is free to love me.

Olivia could see herself as one of the flowers she worked with everyday with their meager beginnings. The beauty is that with the right kind of nourishment they have the opportunity to thrive and prosper. She had been nourished today. Olivia could feel the love blooming and blossoming in her now fertile soul.

God IS good! He WAS listening.

Olivia couldn't wait to call Jack. She was going to invite him for dinner at "her" house tonight.

It will be a dinner prepared with love...a real love that is

filled with passion, joy, and energy that is complete without

fear.

Olivia's Journal

My self-imposed estrangement from God came to a sudden termination today. It was because of one sentence my minister said in her sermon today. Rejuvenation has replaced my malaise. Jack is coming for dinner tonight. The menu will be divine with Jack's tastes in mind. It will be a great evening!

Rachael was in my dreams last night. She was sitting on a window seat in a bay window. She was smiling and looking content. There were so many other people trying to get to her as well. It was hard to break through the crowd to speak to her. It felt right to jump over the crowd, yelling out, "We all miss you so much! Are you happy?"

Rachael smiled and said, "Yes, very happy!"

"That's so great to know, Rachael! *I* am happy, too!" Rachael's nostril was quivering as she laughed and said, "That's so wonderful, Olivia!"

I yelled back and said what I should have told her many years before, "I love the way your right nostril quivers when you laugh real hard. It's so cute!"

I am listening now...

I read some words today from an Eskimo legend that gave me even more comfort:

Perhaps they are not the stars, but rather openings in heaven where the love of our lost ones pours through and shines down upon us to let us know they are happy.

The Tapestry

Olivia and Jack were sitting on the patio eating dinner when Jack abruptly said, "Olivia, didn't you once tell me that you loved little, yellow houses? I saw one for sale today."

Startled, Olivia looked up at him and said, "Yes, how did you remember that?"

"I was listening," Jack said.

He's been listening!

Olivia looked up into those sweet, brown eyes. She knew at that moment that Jack was her home, and she was his. She knew he was the man she had loved in her soul before he had even stepped into her life. Olivia felt her heart being touched as waves of comforting warmth and security blanketed her. It took her back to the time when she had felt her most safe and secure lying in her bed as a child listening to her parents discussing their day.

"I love you, Jack," Olivia said for the first time as her heart opened wide.

"I love you, too, Olivia," said Jack.

"Let's go look at that little, yellow house. It needs someone to love and care for it, too," said Jack.

Olivia suddenly heard the flutter of wings. She looked up to see the mourning dove, her constant companion of late, soaring over the treetops with a full wingspread as if to say, "Goodbye for now. You are whole!"

Goodbye! I'm going to be just fine!

Olivia could almost hear her father saying, just as he had so many years before, "You look mighty pretty today. I'm so proud of you!"

I will make you even prouder. *I* have given myself the great gift of love. *I* am listening to you now!

Olivia's Journal

*J*ack and *I* are happily married now and living in that charming, little, yellow house. That's perfect, because *I* just happen to be a charming, little, yellow house where happy things happen on the inside. *G*od is living here with me now. *I* glanced over the rail from the upstairs balcony and glimpsed a wide band of bright sunshine in the foyer. Sparkling in the glow, I could have sworn *I* saw *H*is suitcases in the foyer.

I feel comforted.
I feel peaceful.
I feel safe.

Death is nothing at all; I have only slipped away into the next room. I am I, and you are you; whatever we were to each other, that we still are. Call me by my old familiar name, speak to me in the easy way you always used. Put no difference into your tone, wear no forced air of solemnity or sorrow. Laugh as we always laughed at the little jokes we enjoyed together. Play, smile, think of me, pray for me. Life means all that it ever meant. It is the same as it always was; there is absolutely unbroken continuity. I am but waiting for you, for an interval, somewhere very near, just around the corner...All is well.

Sir Henry Scott Holland